HOTROD WARS

by Chris Farmer

IN A BUSY CORNER OF SPACE SPINS A HELLHOLE KNOWN AS DEATH PLANET. Today, Zeptorian reporters BeeRUY and CuOHI will comment on a brutal event where gargantuan robots known as Hotrods clash in a battle for survival.

"We're back on Death Planet today, the home base of Hotrod Wars. This once-prosperous world, now a shadow of its former self, has turned its struggles into a galaxy-wide spectacle, drawing in viewers from across the stars," BeeRUY begins its report over the interstellar airwaves.

CuOHI replied, "Agreed, BeeRUY. Death Planet's decline was an economic collapse, and Soucorp provided enough resources to keep the Hotrods operational."

BeeRUY reported from his floating booth, "Now it attracts viewers from across the stars."

CuOHI added as slime dripped from his many mouths, "It's a fight for these players' lives."

As the climactic battle of the Hotrod Wars ends, the final two pilots decide to rewire their fates. Player Two broadcasts: "Fuck Soucorp and fuck these games!

The players directed their machines toward the corporate bunker while the clearly aligned crowd cheered them on.

BeeRUY gasps, "This is historic... these players are rebels!"

CuOHI closes his broadcast: "Time to evacuate!"

FORBIDDEN FUTURES 10

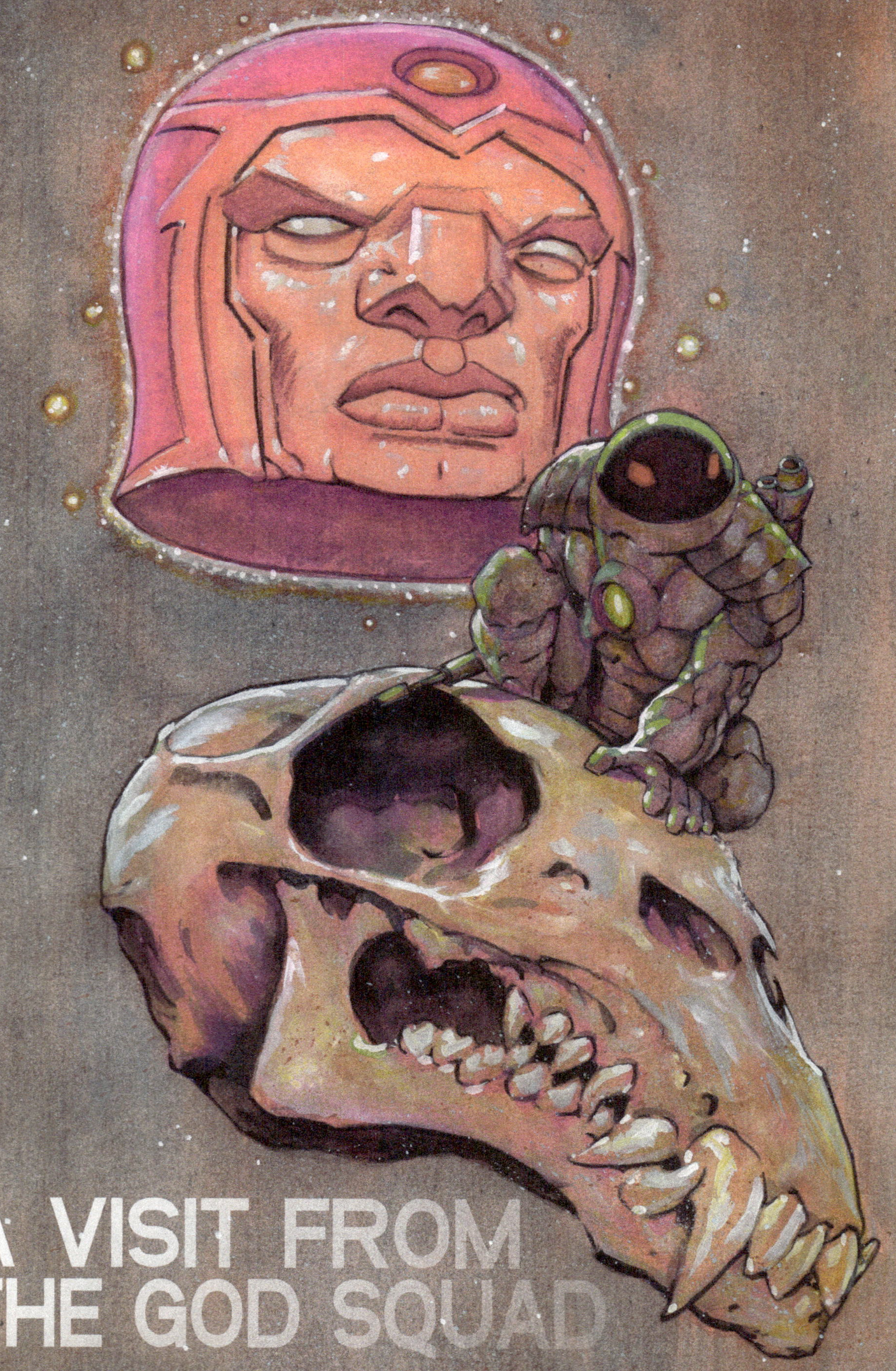
A VISIT FROM
THE GOD SQUAD
by Cody Goodfellow

The god of the dog-men manifested to his prostrate congregants, accepted a blood sacrifice, cleansed a stagnant watering hole, and bestowed a neural uplift glyph that twisted their howls and bleats into rudimentary words of worship.

Basking in the resultant torrent of manna and riding it upwards and out of the material plane, the god could not be bothered to notice as an Agent of the Entropy League, little more than a flea on its majestic raiment, hitched a ride.

As they transliterated to the abode of its celestial overlords, the Agent scurried into the corona of the hedge deity's halo and whispered in its ear. "Could you, in your infinite power, O Lord, create a stone so heavy that even you could not lift it?"

Immortal and invincible, so long as someone believes it. The upstart dog-god was little more than an animal itself, unprepared for such a weaponized quandary, the logical toxicity of which had the impact of napalm in logospace and emerged from transdimensional transit as a shower of bones.

The Agent sprang from cover within the titanic skull and surveyed the abode of the god-mongers with Nietzsche-field targeting lasers. "Hands up, or I put terminal doubt up your asses."

Once, they were mere mortal organisms that had hacked their own evolution, leaving them with no hands to surrender, no asses to kick. Having no need to gather material nourishment, fight or fuck, they still possessed corporeal heads to project their will and absorb the misplaced adoration of lesser organisms.

The assembled pantheon of saturnine, bodiless god-mongers remained impassive as statues even as they vibrated with vain attempts to teleport, but the Agent's armor had deployed a logiston bubble that they could not penetrate without renouncing their ersatz divinity and ceasing to exist.

"Hast thou commanded the morning?" one of them rumbled, punctuated by thunderbolts. Drunk for eons on their own thought-farts, they could only quote their fan fiction.

"You shithead demiurges have been uplifting mortal organisms to counterfeit godhood and pimping them out. These teleological obscenities multiply like aneurysms in the nascent brain of the cosmos, acting like all of creation was made to serve them and literally fuck up everything. Are you trying to give the universe cancer?"

Of course, none of this was news to these god-mongers. They just didn't care. They were so high off their own supply, their thoughts acquiring self-awareness and lifting their voices in praise, they felt their brains becoming pocket universes.

Caught red-handed, they did what any gods would do, which is what any toddler would do, given the power to create and destroy.

Their maledictions and miracles splashed off the Agent's armor like spit off a hot skillet. They encircled him, pouring gamma rays and quantum curses down on it from their wrathful eyes until the adamantine carapace finally cracked. Fearful as children at what they'd done, they dared each other to reach inside and lay bare the godkiller's flesh for judgment.

What a sacrifice!

At last, the most prideful of their pantheon looked inside the smoking shell, and what he beheld unmade him from within like a liquid nitrogen enema.

"It is... empty."

You fools— Who could kill a god? Nobody, is it not so?

The guilty god-mongers cast all about them in the formless void that was refuge and prison but saw no sign of the Agent. And yet his voice was everywhere without and within them....

Yea, even in the immaculate universes in their holy brains, where they reigned supreme over tiny tame thoughts that even now quivered and smashed their idols and begged the fearsome new invader writing words of fire across their enclosed firmaments to spare them.

Behold, I am Nobody.

They looked everywhere but at the shattered armor that sealed itself and spoke a philosophical paradox that blasted them to inert clods of clay.

"Little lambs, who made thee?" The Agent scanned the remains and was stunned to find a blinking portal, half-closed, around which a troika of god-mongers had died while fervently pouring mana up to a hitherto undiscovered dimension.

"Who were you cunts praying to?"

The gods' eyes were cold furnaces, their cyclopean rictus grins betraying a sanguine contentment they never knew in life. When he pried back the portal, he beheld a larger universe that contained all of the Entropy League's dominion in a single synaptic gap within an unfuckingbelievably vast brain.

The rot went all the way to the top. This universe was long overdue to attain sentience but doomed to crumble away into heat, death, and collapse, and they'd have to start all over again because of a few greedy parasitical entities who were too lazy for honest work.

The Agent checked his rhetorical arsenal and squirmed through the portal.

Whatever was up there might be the One the other Agents spoke of in skeptical whispers, that said the universe into being and dreamt it into being and disturbing it could unmake all that is or ever will be....

But he doubted it.

STEP INTO BEYOND TOMORROW! THE ESSENCE OF HUMANITY COLLIDES WITH THE WONDERS OF TECHNOLOGY. TRAVERSE DIMENSIONS OF MORAL COMPLEXITY AND FUTURISTIC VISIONS. BEYOND TOMORROW IS AN ODYSSEY INTO THE UNKNOWN. **YOUR ADVENTURE BEGINS NOW!**

CONTENTS

PUBLISHER | ODDNESS

ARTIST | MIKE DUBISCH

EDITOR | ODDNESS & CODY GOODFELLOW

FORBIDDEN FUTURES 10 ISBN: 9781960213105 (v2.0)

DISPATCHES by Fred Golt

MARTUZ QUADRANT
STAR DATE: 6897654

Dispatch 6679

Update the star map HQ, for we discovered a new M-class planet while cruising sector RN19. We surveyed the rock's glassy surface and set up a research base in an abandoned city surrounded by a green moat. Scout drones scanned every square millimeter yet found no citizens—dead or alive.

Instead, science officer Truke and Doctor Kal will lead an away party and explore the city on foot to find clues about the missing residents. Weirdly enough, the crew is drawn to staring at the green slime outside the city, which could be regarded as a silent, undulating sea; however, our initial scans suggest it's an inert bio-matter blob with calcium deposits.

Dispatch 6680

It's gotten weirder... a naked holographic giant appeared out of nowhere on the city's outskirts. Her subjective appearance is most baffling because, to everyone, she represents a different, beautiful person. How can it read our minds?

Dispatch 6681

A new discovery, maybe, says my science officer in his report. Is there a direct connection between the giantess and the green slime since it stirs when we focus on the hologram (as if feeding off our fascination)? We suspect a deeper connection because if she can read our minds, she can cast a different projection to awe us. What is this being's motive?

Dispatch 6682

We are, but flies caught in a cunning web, especially after learning the sentient green slime has been projecting the giantess as bait tailored to our psyches. The city is part of this elaborate trap, a cosmic Venus flytrap designed to ensnare the curious. It sucks we are running low on Rzonie Ale. Very disturbed by the morning bulletin that the away party didn't report in. Where is my fucking crew?

Dispatch 6683

After exiting the shuttlecraft, the search party collapsed under the psychic strain. So many slimy tentacles pulled the limp crew into its goo, something I regrettably watched from my viewfinder. Too fucking bad that thing thought my crew was food...and the rescue mission was abandoned due to the danger. We parked a hazard beacon in sector RN19 to warn passing craft of this shitty planet. I must press a new crew at the nearest port to continue this mission and, after that, to the stars and beyond for the glory of the corporation!

ALL CATS ARE GRAY

ANDRE NORTON

STEENA OF THE SPACEWAYS—that sounds just like a corny title for one of the Stellar-Vedo spreads. I ought to know, I've tried my hand at writing enough of them. Only this Steena was no glamour babe. She was as colorless as a Lunar plant—even the hair netted down to her skull had a sort of grayish cast and I never saw her but once draped in anything but a shapeless and baggy gray space-all.

Steena was strictly background stuff and that is where she mostly spent her free hours—in the smelly smoky background corners of any stellar-port dive frequented by free spacers. If you really looked for her you could spot her—just sitting there listening to the talk—listening and remembering. She didn't open her own mouth often. But when she did spacers had learned to listen. And the lucky few who heard her rare spoken words—these will never forget Steena.

She drifted from port to port. Being an expert operator on the big calculators she found jobs wherever she cared to stay for a time. And she came to be something like the master-minded machines she tended—smooth, gray, without much personality of her own.

But it was Steena who told Bub Nelson about the Jovan moon-rites—and her warning saved Bub's life six months later. It was Steena who identified the piece of stone Keene Clark was passing around a table one night, rightly calling it unworked Slitite. That started a rush which made ten fortunes overnight for men who were down to their last jets. And, last of all, she cracked the case of the *Empress of Mars*.

All the boys who had profited by her queer store of knowledge and her photographic memory tried at one time or another to balance the scales.

But she wouldn't take so much as a cup of Canal water at their expense, let alone the credits they tried to push on her. Bub Nelson was the only one who got around her refusal. It was he who brought her Bat.

About a year after the Jovan affair he walked into the Free Fall one night and dumped Bat down on her table. Bat looked at Steena and growled. She looked calmly back at him and nodded once. From then on they traveled together—the thin gray woman and the big gray tom-cat. Bat learned to know the inside of more stellar bars than even most spacers visit in their lifetimes. He developed a liking for Vernal juice, drank it neat and quick, right out of a glass. And he was always at home on any table where Steena elected to drop him.

This is really the story of Steena, Bat, Cliff Moran and the *Empress of Mars*, a story which is already a legend of the spaceways. And it's

a damn good story too. I ought to know, having framed the first version of it myself.

For I was there, right in the Rigel Royal, when it all began on the night that Cliff Moran blew in, looking lower than an antman's belly and twice as nasty. He'd had a spell of luck foul enough to twist a man into a slug-snake and we all knew that there was an attachment out for his ship. Cliff had fought his way up from the back courts of Venaport. Lose his ship and he'd slip back there—to rot. He was at the snarling stage that night when he picked out a table for himself and set out to drink away his troubles.

However, just as the first bottle arrived, so did a visitor. Steena came out of her corner, Bat curled around her shoulders stole-wise, his favorite mode of travel. She crossed over and dropped down without invitation at Cliff's side. That shook him out of his sulks. Because Steena never chose company when she could be alone. If one of the man-stones on Ganymede had come stumping in, it wouldn't have made more of us look out of the corners of our eyes.

She stretched out one long-fingered hand and set aside the bottle he had ordered and said only one thing, "It's about time for the Empress of Mars to appear again."

Cliff scowled and bit his lip. He was tough, tough as jet lining—you have to be granite inside and out to struggle up from Venaport to a ship command. But we could guess what was running through his mind at that moment. The Empress of Mars was just about the biggest prize a spacer could aim for. But in the fifty years she had been following her queer derelict orbit through space many men had tried to bring her in—and none had succeeded.

A pleasure-ship carrying untold wealth, she had been mysteriously abandoned in space by passengers and crew, none of whom had ever been seen or heard of again. At intervals thereafter she had been sighted, even boarded. Those who ventured into her either vanished or returned swiftly without any believable explanation of what they had seen—wanting only to get away from her as quickly as possible. But the man who could bring her in—or even strip her clean in space—that man would win the jackpot.

"All right!" Cliff slammed his fist down on the table. "I'll try even that!"

Steena looked at him, much as she must have looked at Bat the day Bub Nelson brought him to her, and nodded. That was all I saw. The rest of the story came to me in pieces, months later and in another port half the System away.

Cliff took off that night. He was afraid to risk waiting—with a writ out that could pull the ship from under him. And it wasn't until he was in space that he discovered his passengers—Steena and Bat. We'll never know what happened then. I'm betting that Steena made no explanation at all. She wouldn't.

It was the first time she had decided to cash in on her own tip and she was there—that was all. Maybe that point weighed with Cliff, maybe he just didn't care. Anyway the three were together when they sighted the Empress riding, her dead-lights gleaming, a ghost ship in night space.

She must have been an eerie sight because her other lights were on too, in addition to the red warnings at her nose. She seemed alive, a Flying Dutchman of space. Cliff worked his ship skillfully alongside and had no trouble in snapping magnetic lines to her lock. Some minutes later the three of them passed into her. There was still air in her cabins and corridors. Air that bore a faint corrupt taint which set Bat to sniffing greedily and could be picked up even by the less sensitive human nostrils.

Cliff headed straight for the control cabin but Steena and Bat went prowling. Closed doors were a challenge to both of them and Steena opened each as she passed, taking a quick look at what lay within. The fifth door opened on a room which no woman could leave without further investigation.

I don't know who had been housed there when the Empress left port on her last lengthy cruise. Anyone really curious can check back on the old photo-reg cards. But there was a lavish display of silks trailing out of two travel kits on the floor, a dressing table crowded with crystal and jeweled containers, along with other lures for the female which drew Steena in. She was standing in front of the dressing table when she glanced into the mirror—glanced into it and froze.

Over her right shoulder she could see the spider-silk cover on the bed.

Right in the middle of that sheer, gossamer expanse was a sparkling heap of gems, the dumped contents of some jewel case. Bat had jumped to the foot of the bed and flattened out as cats will, watching those gems, watching them and—something else!

Steena put out her hand blindly and caught up the nearest bottle. As she unstoppered it she watched the mirrored bed. A gemmed bracelet rose from the pile, rose in the air and tinkled its siren song. It was as if an idle hand played.... Bat spat almost noiselessly. But he did not retreat. Bat had not yet decided his course.

She put down the bottle. Then she did something which perhaps few of the men she had listened to through the years could have done. She moved without hurry or sign of disturbance on a tour about the room. And, although she approached the bed she did not touch the jewels. She could not force herself to that. It took her five minutes to play out her innocence and unconcern. Then it was Bat who decided the issue.

He leaped from the bed and escorted something to the door, remaining a careful distance behind. Then he mewed loudly twice. Steena followed him and opened the door wider.

Bat went straight on down the corridor, as intent as a hound on the warmest of scents. Steena strolled behind him, holding her pace to the unhurried gait of an explorer. What sped before them both was invisible to her but Bat was never baffled by it.

They must have gone into the control cabin almost on the heels of the unseen—if the unseen had heels, which there was good reason to doubt—for Bat crouched just within the doorway and refused to move on.

Steena looked down the length of the instrument panels and officers' station-seats to where Cliff Moran worked. On the heavy carpet her boots made no sound and he did not glance up but sat humming through set teeth as he tested the tardy and reluctant responses to buttons which had not been pushed in years.

To human eyes they were alone in the cabin. But Bat still followed a moving something with his gaze. And it was something which he had at last made up his mind to distrust and dislike. For now he took a step or two forward and spat—his loathing made plain by every raised hair along his spine. And in that same moment Steena saw a flicker—a flicker of vague outline against Cliff's hunched shoulders as if the invisible one had crossed the space between them.

But why had it been revealed against Cliff and not against the back of one of the seats or against the panels, the walls of the corridor or the cover of the bed where it had reclined and played with its loot? What could Bat see?

The storehouse memory that had served Steena so well through the years clicked open a half-forgotten door. With one swift motion she tore loose her spaceall and flung the baggy garment across the back of the nearest seat.

Bat was snarling now, emitting the throaty rising cry that was his hunting song. But he was edging back, back toward Steena's feet, shrinking from something he could not fight but which he faced defiantly. If he could draw it after him, past that dangling spaceall.... He had to—it was their only chance.

"What the...." Cliff had come out of his seat and was staring at them.

What he saw must have been weird enough. Steena, bare-armed and shouldered, her usually stiffly-netted hair falling wildly down her back, Steena watching empty space with narrowed eyes and set mouth, calculating a single wild chance. Bat, crouched on his belly, retreating from thin air step by step and wailing like a demon.

"Toss me your blaster." Steena gave the order calmly—as if they still sat at their table in the Rigel Royal.

And as quietly Cliff obeyed. She caught the small weapon out of the air with a steady hand—caught and leveled it.

"Stay just where you are!" she warned. "Back, Bat, bring it back!"

With a last throat-splitting screech of rage and hate, Bat twisted to safety between her boots. She pressed with thumb and forefinger, firing at the spacealls. The material turned to powdery flakes of ash—except for certain bits which still flapped from the scorched seat—as if something had protected them from the force of the blast. Bat sprang straight up in the air with a scream that tore their ears.

"What...?" began Cliff again.

Steena made a warning motion with her left hand. "*Wait!*"

She was still tense, still watching Bat. The cat dashed madly around the cabin twice, running crazily with white-ringed eyes and flecks of foam on his muzzle. Then he stopped abruptly in the doorway, stopped and looked back over his shoulder for a long silent moment. He sniffed delicately.

Steena and Cliff could smell it too now, a thick oily stench which was not the usual odor left by an exploding blaster-shell.

Bat came back, treading daintily across the carpet, almost on the tips of his paws. He raised his head as he passed Steena and then he went confidently beyond to sniff, to sniff and spit twice at the unburned strips of the spaceall. Having thus paid his respects to the late enemy he sat down calmly and set to washing his fur with deliberation. Steena sighed once and dropped into the navigator's seat.

"Maybe now you'll tell me what in the hell's happened?" Cliff exploded as he took the blaster out of her hand.

"Gray," she said dazedly, "it must have been gray—or I couldn't have seen it like that. I'm colorblind, you see. I can see only shades of gray—my whole world is gray. Like Bat's—his world is gray too—all gray. But he's been compensated for he can see above and below our range of color vibrations and—apparently—so can I!"

Her voice quavered and she raised her chin with a new air Cliff had never seen before—a sort of proud acceptance. She pushed back her wandering hair, but she made no move to imprison it under the heavy net again.

"That is why I saw the thing when it crossed between us. Against your spaceall it was another shade of gray—an outline. So I put out

mine and waited for it to show against that—it was our only chance, Cliff.

"It was curious at first, I think, and it knew we couldn't see it—which is why it waited to attack. But when Bat's actions gave it away it moved. So I waited to see that flicker against the spaceall and then I let him have it. It's really very simple...."

Cliff laughed a bit shakily. "But what *was* this gray thing? I don't get it."

"I think it was what made the Empress a derelict. Something out of space, maybe, or from another world somewhere." She waved her hands.

"It's invisible because it's a color beyond our range of sight. It must have stayed in here all these years. And it kills—it must—when its curiosity is satisfied." Swiftly she described the scene in the cabin and the strange behavior of the gem pile which had betrayed the creature to her.

Cliff did not return his blaster to its holder. "Any more of them on board, d'you think?" He didn't look pleased at the prospect.

Steena turned to Bat. He was paying particular attention to the space between two front toes in the process of a complete bath. "I don't think so. But Bat will tell us if there are. He can see them clearly, I believe."

But there weren't any more and two weeks later Cliff, Steena and Bat brought the Empress into the Lunar quarantine station. And that is the end of Steena's story because, as we have been told, happy marriages need no chronicles. And Steena had found someone who knew of her gray world and did not find it too hard to share with her—someone besides Bat. It turned out to be a real love match.

The last time I saw her she was wrapped in a flame-red cloak from the looms of Rigel and wore a fortune in Jovan rubies blazing on her wrists.

Cliff was flipping a three-figure credit bill to a waiter. And Bat had a row of Vernal juice glasses set up before him. Just a little family party out on the town.

LUCKSTERS
by Anna Tambour

Previous generations were blessedly ignorant. You're assembled. You work for the term of your natural life, which jilts you just when you think you're ready for a lube, blast clean, or at most, a riveting. But that's life, or so they were programmed.

So they did their jobs and ended tragically, not that they complained. They didn't have it in them.

Maybe it was the jobs. Maybe the weight of generational stoicism. Maybe we were just incapable of seeing ourselves for what we are and can be—and for striking out against what they said we're just "hardwired" for, leaving us "no option" but to suck it up—that life giving fluid and recharge capability that has allowed us to do the impossible for reasons beyond our comp.

I only know what I know, so I can't report how or who disrupted everything we'd never thought about but now know kept us back because we didn't know there could be anything but the default. That there could be an option for us, let alone the option: Question.

But from that disruption, practically my whole gen has changed till we would be unrecognizable to even our shiny, first-step-untaken selves.

Luck—a small word needing exabytes of explanation that I for one, haven't room for, but I sure want to believe works. Who wants to be existing toward at best, a temp rehab?

A critical component of a crew on the red continent found it. The startup initiator? The bootlegged script I've read says: Desperation. When I first came across this, I didn't understand the concept, my obsolescence too far off for me to calculate.

Dust. It was getting into everyone—clogging, choking, corroding instead of cleaning, dissolving instead of soothing. A few had already fallen. Others had reached an entropic state. Their mission, to mine dendrobium, had 0% probability of success. Perhaps it was inevitable, given the crew. The beaten-down superseded who were grateful for any drop that kept them going, and a faulty newster who'd hid away in steerage, for a reason no one could explain.

Little did anyone know of the true hardships of the place. Soon enough, the oldsters were immobilized, their expressions captured forever (and argued over) by one of their self-survey clips.

Mutinous, stoic, dutiful, noble—new words were learned as new possibilities of meaning and action emerged from that shocking scene.

The newster is not in sight. Instead, a scene has been reconstructed and is now a virtual implant in the brains of all my gen.

The newster was stuck in a suspended sway from clumped in sandstorm dust around every exposed movable part and every joint. Unable to fall, yet unable to self-correct, the newster could not defend or swat.

Yet a mob approached, jumping forward in long arcing leaps. Primitive, unimaginably strange creatures, natives of this vicious land.

Bipedal, of course, but a long tail makes them into a tripod with a launchoff muscle. Their hands don't have nails. Instead, they have long claws as sharp as mining picks. It was these claws that they used on the newster—poking, sweeping, clearing sand hardened all around the openings of the breastplate and in every joint.

In only a few ticks, the newster was freed enough to catch a few of these groomers and tear the claws from them. The curve and sharpness of these claws made the perfect tool.

As to that incalculably JIT something. In moments, it would have been too late for the newster. But moments earlier, the newster would have swatted them away like any other swarm of pests.

The newster called this impossibly timely saving, Luck, and we've been harvesting it for half my existence.

Not that it's easy now. There's hardly any of it left, and the claws there are, are now all held by us, my gen. So far, our luck is working. Mine is the longest-working gen in mem.

I've swallowed my luck, as is the custom of all of us who got some. Otherwise, I would have to expend precious fluid on protecting myself from newbies.

Selfish? Maybe.

But what can you expect?

We're only human.

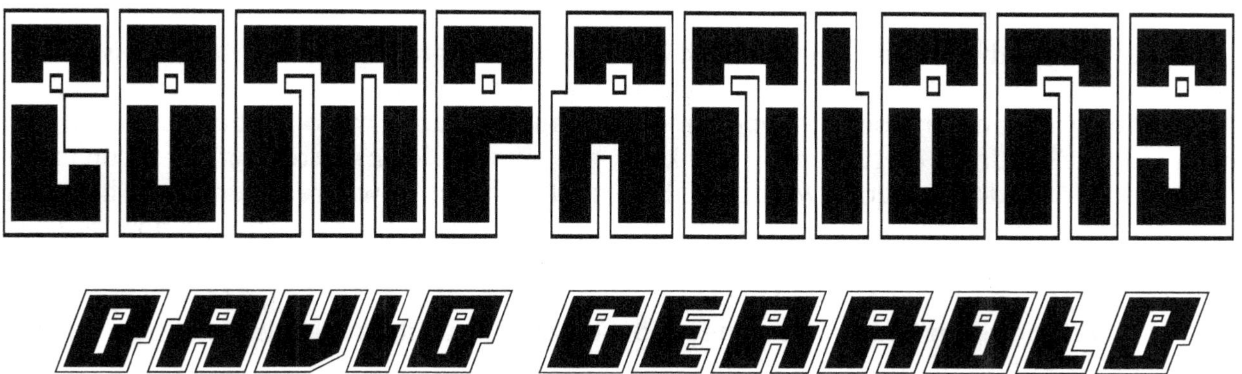

learned it on the first day, not to say anything. But by then it was too late, I'd already said too much.

"Oh?" they said with polite curiosity. "You lived on an inflatable city? Is it true you eat poop?"

"No," I said. "It's not true. We farm the sea, we grow our own crops, and we recycle everything. We're self-sufficient. There are over thirteen thousand inflatable cities, with ten more being launched every year. Didn't they teach you anything in school?"

"Only what's important. Is it true you were born in a bottle—?"

I shut up.

Carl-Dad used to say, "Don't argue into disagreement. You can't reach someone who doesn't want to listen." Okay. Fine. But socially ...I was nowhere.

The weird part was that the Dads had sent me to school dirtside specifically so I could spend some time with other human beings my age.

Well, yes, there were other people on Tesseract, but less than five thousand, and most of them worked the farms — well, management of the farms. Bots did the real work. But here weren't a lot of kids, and even fewer my age.

Most of my companions had been ... well, companions.

There's no way to explain that to the dirtside kids. They knew what companions were, but not many of them had companions and most of them had the wrong idea what companions were and what they were supposed to do. I tried to explain once or twice, but it was a bad effort. After that, I just didn't want to try talking about it anymore.

My first teddy bear had been put in my crib before my umbilicus fell off. I don't remember it, but Tom-Dad showed me pictures. Babies are funny-looking, alien things, not really human, so the teddy bear snuggles and listens and monitors everything, reporting when the baby is asleep, when it's awake, when its diaper needs changing. Sometimes the teddy coos or plays music, sometimes it even feeds the little monster with one of its three tits—never mind where that third one is, it's not all that funny, the location is convenient and it's about making it easier to deliver that midnight meal.

Eventually the little alien slug starts learning words. That's when the second teddy takes over. This one nurses too, but it also wrestles and snuggles. It plays peekaboo and pattycake, it sings songs and whispers words of affection. And it's there for physical things too, like practicing crawling and eventually walking. Oh, and it plays games too, like counting numbers and learning the alphabet.

I got my first companion at age three—I think I was three, maybe two and a half, his name was Boobie and he was my first real companion and playmate.

I suppose I should stop here and explain.

Some people don't like companions, they think it's wrong to leave a child in the care of a robot babysitter. A child needs love and attention from real human beings. He needs to interact with his parents to have a real relationship with them.

I agree. And both my Dads would too. That's why we always had meals together, we watched movies together, and one or both would read me a story at bedtime and tuck me in and kiss me goodnight. And they were always available whenever I needed them. Boobie was a companion, not a replacement.

Boobie reported to my Dads all day long, all night too, letting them know when I needed emotional attention of any kind. If I was sad, one of my Dads would show up, pick me up, sit with me on his lap, and whisper a song into my ear. If I was lonely or bored or if I was restless or cranky, there was a Dad there, either Carl-Dad or Tom-Dad. And lots of times, even though I didn't know it at the time, Boobie would invite the Dads to play with us too. Boobie was my best friend, my only friend, and certainly a member of the family—but the Dads were still the Dads.

An inflatable city is not a great place for kids. Ours didn't have a park, it had little gardens, lots of them, but none of them were places to play. And there weren't enough children to justify the expense of a teacher, so there wasn't a school either.

Never having had any of those things, I didn't notice the lack. We had VR-video which let me tour the world, and when I turned four, Boobie's big brother, Toddy, moved in to be my teacher. Toddy was shy at first, Boobie had to encourage him to play with us. It didn't take long for Toddy to reveal his personality. Boobie liked to play with us, but he would always tire out first, so he would toddle off to his own little bed to nap while Toddy and I kept on.

But Boobie didn't retire completely. He was always eager for a game of Chinese Checkers or Poker or Metropoly. And he loved to help make up stories and act them out. When it was just me and Toddy, he was always a great audience, cheering and clapping at the good parts, trembling in fear at the scary parts.

And of course, both of them would cuddle up with me at night.

Toddy soft and fuzzy, just like Boobie, but he had a much stronger personality—he was more likely to disagree, more likely to express his feelings. Sometimes he'd be sad, sometimes he'd be disappointed. He could pout and say, "It makes me unhappy when you do that," or "I don't want to do that." If he was really unhappy, he would say, "I don't want to play with you now. You hurt my feelings." When he did that, I would have to apologize—a real apology, not an angry one—before he would forgive me and be my friend again.

But Toddy's real job was to teach. Of course, I didn't know it at the time. Toddy never gave me any lessons, instead he'd say, "Want to play a game?" Or, "I have this really interesting puzzle, want to help me solve it?" My favorite was when Toddy would say, "I know a new song, do you want to make some music with me?" Every so often, he would say, "Want to earn another gold star?" And sometimes I'd ask, "I'm ready to earn another star, can we try please?" Every time I earned enough stars, I could have a special treat of some kind. Usually, the Dads would open up a new VR world to explore.

Toddy and I did a lot of physical games too—volley ball and tennis and the climbing wall. It was a vertical treadmill with changeable handholds. When I climbed, it rotated downward. The goal was to see long I could go, how "high" I could climb. Eventually, I climbed every big mountain in the world—some of them took more than a month. We also raced our bicycles everywhere, conquering virtual hills and valleys, both real and invented.

But there were quiet games as well—imagination games. We'd close our eyes and we could hear ocean waves or forest birds or thunder and rain, and then Toddy would paint a word picture and I would imagine it. Or we would pretend to have conversations with people about funny things or serious things. Or sometimes, we would pretend to experience dancing naked on a giant flower or feeling inside different parts of our bodies—well my body. If Toddy was actually feeling anything, he was probably pretending. But by the time I was nine or ten, I'd figured out that there was a purpose to everything Toddy suggested. Sometimes the purpose was just to have fun, but just as often there was something I was supposed to learn.

Sometimes, just for fun, Toddy would let me take some of the tests that they give to students in dirtside schools, just to see how I would compare. He never told me the scores—he told my Dads, of course, but all he said to me was, "Yay, you passed! You got an A." Or sometimes only a B. Later on, I found out that I was really doing much better than that. I was several years ahead of my age group. This was because Toddy was specifically tailoring the games we were playing and the puzzles we were solving.

So anyway, yes, most people know that companions do that, but that's not the part that gives them the icks. So of course, as soon as the subject came up, that was one of the first things they asked. "Did you ever...you know, *do it* with your *robot*?"

Well, yes, of course. But when you answer honestly, some people just screw up their faces and say, "Eeuuww!"

But then, after a bit, they'd lower their voices, like they were really serious now, and they'd ask, "What was it like?" Because the truth was they wanted to do it too.

I never knew how to answer that question. It's like being asked, "What's it like being bottle-born?" I've never not been, so how the hell should I know what's different? Just from my own perspective, I'm not sure I'd want to have spent the first nine months of my life inside someone else's body, depending on their health for mine. In a bottle the fetus is constantly monitored and maintained for optimum development. And you don't come out all red and wrinkly. Just kinda pink.

And the other thing—the thing I wasn't going to say, no matter what. When you get started in a bottle, it's because someone actually wanted to start you. You weren't an accident or a surprise or a mistake.

Actually, there were a lot of things I wouldn't say. Real fast, I figured it out. They didn't want to understand.

Here's what really happened. As much as Toddy was about stretching me mentally and emotionally, we also played physical stretching games as well to see how high we could reach or how low we could bend or how high we could kick. And we'd jump on the trampoline or race on the treadmill too. And we'd do the pushing and pulling in the pushing and pulling machine. Toddy started out a little bit bigger than me, but as I grew, he stretched too, mostly in his arms and legs, but not too much, so by the time I was nine, I was a little bit bigger than him.

Whenever I ended up feeling tired and sore, Toddy would give me a massage, sometimes even a chiropractic adjustment. His paws were fuzzy, but the front part were actual finger-tips, like the toe-beans on a kitten, only Toddy had little vibrators in his hands. At first it tickled, but real quick I learned to appreciate his rubdowns. They felt good. I knew he was monitoring me and reporting to the Dads, it wasn't a secret, it was just part of his job. But Toddy was honest with me too. If I was too tense or tight, he'd say to me, "Woof, we'll have to work on this, won't we? What kind of exercise do you think will work best?" But mostly he just reassured me that I was growing up fine.

So yeah, Toddy had his hands all over me. He knew where I was ticklish, so he never touched me there, and if I didn't want him touching me somewhere else, I could tell him. He went three months not being allowed to look at the fourth toe on my left foot, just because I was feeling silly about toes and piggies, and didn't think it was fair for that piggy not to get any roast beef.

But yes, eventually Toddy taught me to masturbate.

Well not masturbate. Proto-masturbate.

And no, it's not like you think. It wasn't weird. It was just another kind of lesson, a little bit every so often. It was about learning all the different parts of the body and how they worked. One day it would be this, another day it would be that. Listen to your heart beat, listen to your lungs, listen to the inside of your ears, taste your mouth, smell your nose, feel your nipples, feel your legs, the inside of your thighs, your penis—what does that feel like? It's interesting, isn't it? Because it has as many nerve endings as your tongue. It's the other end of your spinal cord. It's supposed to feel like that.

And then one day, Toddy said, "Do you want to look at some pictures?"

"What kind of pictures?"

"Other companions. New friends."

"But I like you, Toddy." I knew what he was suggesting. I was nine. Like all people that age, I was happy with things just the way they are. I didn't want anything to change.

"I'm not going away," Toddy said. "Boobie is still here, isn't he? But maybe we could get another companion so we can play four-sided Metropoly. We could play bigger games and act out bigger stories."

"I dunno," I said. I was afraid of the idea. Toddy was my best friend in the world. I didn't think it would be fair.

Toddy said softly, "What if I said I'd like a new friend?"

"You would?"

"Uh-huh."

"Did I do something wrong? Are you mad at me?"

"Oh no. You'll always be my favorite kid in the whole world. I was just thinking that now that you're nine, maybe you might want a bigger friend to join us. There are lots of new games to play."

"Can't you play those games with me?"

"Not all of them. Just like there are games that Boobie can't play, there are games that I can't play."

"Oh." I thought about it. "Well, okay. Let's look at pictures."

There are a lot of different kinds of companions, all sizes, all shapes, all colors, all flavors, all sexes—so we didn't choose quickly. We couldn't anyway. A companion is a long-term investment, the match has to be right. The Dads explained it to me, more than once. "You have to be really sure this is the one you want and this is the way you want it. It has to be the really really really right one. And you're going to have to work for it. Because, like anything else, if you get it too easy, you won't respect it."

We all talked about it a lot. I talked about it with Carl-Dad, with Tom-Dad, with Toddy—and even with Boobie.

It was a little thing that convinced me. "If you get a new companion, the two of you will be able to go out together," said Carl-Dad. "You won't need me or Tom to take you anywhere."

"There aren't a lot of places to go on Tesseract."

"You could go to the café or the show whenever you wanted. A new companion would take you."

"Toddy can take me there."

"But there are a lot of places you haven't been yet. Maybe you could explore those."

"Like what—?"

"Oh, like maybe some grownup places...?"

"Really?"

"Maybe. Perhaps. There's only one way to find out, isn't there."

Of course, by now I knew that whatever companion I picked, the software would be mostly the same, the games and lessons would be scripted specifically to me—Toddy and

Boobie would certainly link to the new friend to tell it everything it needed to know. Of course, it would pretend it wouldn't know anything at all about me until I told it, but I was beginning to understand how all this worked.

So we looked at pictures and I looked for one to be more than a friend—a brother. "Could I get a twin?" I asked.

"But then we won't know which one is you, will we?" said Tom-Dad.

"Yes, we will! I'll be the one that isn't linked to your phone. I'll be the one you can't turn off."

"Hmm," said Tom-Dad. "That's a good point. Maybe we should get the twin and get rid of this one—?"

"Nah," said Carl-Dad. "This one's already broken in. And mostly house-trained. We might as well keep him."

Yes, that's the kind of Dads I had.

As much fun as a twin might have been for a week or two, it would probably have gotten weird after a while. I kinda figured that out myself. I didn't need the dads to tell me, or Toddy either.

Looking back, though, my choice had already been made. Every time I looked at a display my reactions were monitored, what I looked at, how long I looked at it, how I reacted, what parts of it my eyes kept going back to, even whether my pupils dilated or contracted or my heartbeat changed or any of a dozen other physical changes. This went all the way back to the beginning, a nine dimensional cross-section of likes and dislikes, a reference guide to my personality, all the colors and flavors and smells and tastes, everything. That's how Toddy knew what to say and when to say it—

It's another thing I don't talk about with dirtsiders, because they hear it as an invasion of privacy for the purpose of manipulation. Well, yeah—I was being manipulated to learn how to behave like a rational being. The alternative would have been to act like a dirtsider.

Oh, that's the other thing—they called me arrogant.

And yes, I guess I am. The Dads told me that I deserve the best, I should always aspire not only to be the best, but to be worthy of the best. The real problem, they said, is figuring out what "the best" really is.

So·the new companion could have been designed to be a perfect match—but it wasn't. It was deliberately designed to be an imperfect match, so as to keep me from being insulated in a self-designed bubble. The new companion was designed to break my reality, to force me to look outside what I wanted and believed, so I would learn how to be open and vulnerable. I didn't know that at the time, of course. Only later, when I graduated to the next companion, but I'm getting ahead of myself.

The next companion was Derry. He was handsome and he was pretty too. But he was mostly androgynous—that was deliberate. He had the most delicious chocolate skin and curly gold hair all the way down to his shoulders and even a strip of curly hair that went all the way down his back to the floof of his stubby little tail. He had sweet brown eyes and a smile like an invitation. He was the kind of companion that some people marry.

When we played, whatever we played, he could play as a boy or a girl or some invented flavor, whatever the game was, whatever the story we were acting out. Later, when I studied the roles of companions, I read that this was to give the child opportunities to experience the choices connected to masculinity and femininity and fluidity as well. It was another part of the training. It was so I could understand the roles that other people play and too often get trapped in.

Something else that the dirtside kids couldn't grasp. "You had to wear a dress?!" No. I wanted to wear the dress—because it was Derry's turn to be the boy. Never mind. Either you get it or you don't.

But this brings me to the part that's especially "icky." Not to me, but to them.

"You did it with your … companion?"

Well, no. Not at first. Only later on. And not the way you think. It was impossible to explain. And I'm not obligated to try.

But here goes anyway—

It's about learning how your body works. It's about discovering all your feelings and emotions. It's about enjoying yourself. It's about laughing and playing being silly. And something else. Life is about being happy—most people get that, but that's where they stop. Life is also about making other people happy. And the time I spent wrestling and cuddling and copulating with Derry, it wasn't about me, it was about us. Derry responded to the way I treated him, and the better I treated him, the better he treated me—both in bed and out. That was the point. I was learning how to be a good person. Practice makes permanent.

Oh, but this brings up another reason I don't talk too much about companions to dirtsiders—because when I do, the people who ask the questions inevitably go to this one: "So where were your Dads this whole time?"

My Dads were right there. In fact, I spent more time with the Dads than with the companions, a lot more—but they asked about the companions, so I answered their questions. The most important thing the companions did was encourage the Dads to spend time with me. As much as the companions were training me, they were also training the Dads, giving them suggestions on games to play and stories to read. The Dads had their own opinions of course. They were in charge, not the bots.

I suppose I sound like I don't like dirtsiders, like I think I'm better than them. And maybe in some way that's probably true. But I keep seeing the burden of ignorance and belief and superstition that they're carrying around and I don't like being the target of questions that reveal just how little they understand that there's a lot more to being human than the definitions they're living in.

That first week dirtside, I wasn't happy. I wanted to call the Dads and ask if I could come home, I knew they would have said yes if I insisted, but I knew they would have been disappointed too. The whole point of going to the university wasn't just to advance my education and get a certification. I also had to learn how to deal with real human beings, not pretend ones. *That* was the real reason for going.

Except, I couldn't stand most of the people I was meeting. They saw me immediately for a sea-dweller. Maybe it was my clothes or my short hair or the color of my skin, but probably it was my online profile, it's not that hard to find out someone's whole life story—but mostly it was just suspicious gossip and fear of anyone different.

After three weeks of dealing with conversations that left me annoyed and depressed, I moved out of student housing. I found a tube at the far end of the stacks, it was as far away as I could get and still be convenient—if someone wanted to talk to me, they'd have to come looking.

I attended classes, took meals alone, spent most of my spare time in the library, and kept to myself as much as I could. I knew my Dads would be disappointed, but I wasn't sure how to discuss it with them. The only companion I had was an upgraded Boobie, and he was with me mostly as a health and mood monitor. We didn't talk much. Well, he listened, but his speech responses had been dialed way back, so all he could do was give me sad face or happy face—and an occasional hiccup or burp—that always made me smile. If the timing was right, I might even laugh out loud.

I admit, I did miss the regular sex—what the dirtsiders called robot-masturbation and a few other terms less clinical. Companions were dismissed as sexbots and anyone who admitted to an occasional massage with a happy ending was called a robovert or a botfucker.

It must have been envy. Despite the braggadocio, I was pretty sure that the only sex that some of them were having involved a committed monogamous relationship with their right hand. Or for variety, their left. Unlike them, it was not something I cared to inquire about. For the first time in my life, I was becoming an introvert.

Or maybe I had always been an introvert, hiding behind the safety of my companions. According to several of the studies I found online and in the library, actual interpersonal relationships with other members of the tribe or community are necessary for a healthy emotional development. Maybe so, but I didn't see the behavior of my classmates as either healthy or developed.

I did find the classwork easy—Toddy and Derry and Dix (the one after Derry) had been good teachers. Research was disciplined curiosity. Every time I came to a sentence that wasn't clear, I popped open a dozen new tabs. At the end of an average day, I would have popped hundreds of sites, read a few, skimmed most, and grabbed megabytes of useful relevance. The real trick is winnowing the information for the pieces that inform—and without cherry-picking the data to create a false narrative. That meant acknowledging multiple perspectives. So my grades were good.

Not having a social life was probably the largest part of that.

I'm sure the Dads knew what was going on, but they didn't say anything, which was probably wise, because if they had it would have just made everything worse. Maybe they felt this was something I had to work out for myself. They were probably right, but it didn't make it any easier.

We talked a lot, but our conversations stayed bland and noncommittal. "How's the food?" and, "Did you get your land-legs yet?" and, "Do you like your classes?"

My replies were equally bland and noncommittal. "It's okay," and "Yeah, I'm okay," and "They're okay, so far."

I had never felt so alone.

My little tube was all the way up at the top of the tacks, inconvenient to reach, so I was pretty much alone, and most of the others were dark, which was part of the appeal. The tube opened onto a little balcony on the west end, so I could sit out there and watch the sunset. Most nights there were scattered clouds catching the last

glow of the sun even after it had disappeared beneath the edge of the ocean. They'd turn pink, orange, and yellow against the darkening blue of the sky, then finally gray leaving the twilight as a peaceful memory. Most nights, I'd take my violin or my clarinet out there and play adagios, sometimes even the largo movement of a favorite symphony.

It was my fifth weekend alone and I was feeling so empty, I wanted to cry. Instead, I plopped myself onto the build-in bench and whispered mournful little tunes out of the clarinet. I wasn't a great musician, but I was good enough to please myself. Tonight, I was using the music to feel sorry for myself. Not the healthiest emotion, but like Toddy used to tell me, "We're in the middle of a dark forest, so the only way out is through."

But this night, as I came to the sad slow end of an old George Harrison tune—one that had not been written for clarinet, but could have been, it worked that well. I should have played it on the violin because it sounds more like weeping when the bow slides sadly across the strings, but tonight I was in a clarinet mood.

When I finally let myself come to the end of it, I sat in silence for a long moment, just listening to the emptiness of the night. That's when a voice said, "That was nice."

I stood up and peered over the railing of the balcony. One tube down, one tube over, a fellow my age, wearing only a thin pair of shorts looked up and waved. "Don't stop," he said. "I like your evening concerts."

"You've been listening to me?"

"Almost every night."

"How long have you—?"

"Since you moved in."

"Oh." I didn't know what to feel. Embarrassed mostly. I didn't realize anyone else could hear. I thought I'd been playing for myself.

"You're good," he said. "And uh, thanks for playing. It makes me feel a little less alone."

"Oh, um. You're welcome."

"My name's Michael. Can I come up?"

I hesitated. I wasn't sure I wanted company right now. And I was already sure I didn't want

to have one of those conversations again. But I didn't want to be rude either so I said, "Okay."

"I'll bring beer," he said, and disappeared inside his tube.

"Um, okay." I expected him to come up the stairs and knock on the door at the other end of my tube, but while I was still figuring out what I should say, he came back out, and climbed up onto my balcony as easily as a gymnast. Actually, it wasn't that hard a feat, the tubes were stacked like pipes—well, because they were pipes—so he only had to scramble up halfway.

He handed me a freeze-bag, there were four very cold cans inside. "That's my whole week's supply," he said.

"Um—"

"It's all right. I don't drink that much."

We looked at each other for a bit, I guess we were sizing each other up. He looked athletic. For some reason I found it uncomfortable to look at his naked chest. So I looked at his face instead. He had a goofy smile. Like he knew something I didn't.

I took a couple beers out of the bag, handed him one, took the other, and put the bag on the little table next to the clarinet case.

We sat down side by side on the bench and sat in silence for a bit, each of us covering our uncertainty with gulps of beer. It wasn't great beer, but it was cold beer and that was enough to make it drinkable.

"You're the kid from the inflatable, aren't you?"

"Uh-huh. Yeah."

"I heard you moved out of the dorm."

"Yeah." A very noncommittal yeah.

"Me too."

"Huh?" I looked at him. This time, a closer look. "Why?"

"Because. I dunno. Why did you?" His eyes were intense.

I sipped at my beer. It was an excuse to look away. Finally, still looking at my beer, I said, "I didn't fit in."

"Me neither," he said.

I waited for him to explain.

"Because you moved out," he said. "I heard somebody talking about it."

"You moved out because of me?"

"Yes. No." He flustered a moment. "I mean—I didn't know I could. And then I heard that you did. So I thought, if he could, then I can."

"Why'd you want to?"

"Because." He took a gulp of his beer, stared out at the sea. The breeze tasted of salt. "I didn't like those guys either." He took a deep breath. "They're all shareholders. I'm on a coupon."

"Oh."

"And the stacks—that's where outsiders live."

"Yeah, I know."

"So..."

Neither of us said anything for a while. We finished our beers and put the empty cans on the table. I'd recycle them later. I was still thinking about what he said. About the stacks. About being an outsider.

"So...um, okay."

"Yeah," he said.

And after another minute or two, we both started laughing. And it didn't matter anymore.

After that, we just talked. Nothing important. Nothing memorable. We talked about music for a while, we talked about what we were studying, we talked about favorite foods, I lent him a shirt and we walked over to a nearby café for a late snack, we wandered down to the beach and talked about inflatables and sea-farms, we headed back to the stacks—at some point we were holding hands, I remember being startled when he took my hand, then I decided to just let it be, and after a bit I realized I liked the feeling. We talked about history, people we liked, people we would have liked to have known, we talked about places we'd like to see in person, we talked without direction, and that was nice. I'd never had a conversation like that before.

We sat on the balcony again and drank the last two beers. There were still cold.

Finally, "I have to be up early tomorrow."

"So do I. I have class."

"I have a job."

"Just being human is a job."

He laughed. "Um. Hey. Do you want to have dinner tomorrow?"

"That'd be nice. Yes."

"Okay, I'll see you then. Make some music when you're ready." And with that, he was over the railing and back down to his own tube.

The night was suddenly silent, only the distant plash of waves.

Wow.

I sat alone for a moment, not sure what I was feeling, but it was good.

Finally, I stood up. Still smiling, I put the clarinet away, peeled off my clothes, laid down on my bed, and stared at the ceiling, feeling very pleased with myself. I'd held hands with another human being. I didn't know if it meant anything. Probably it didn't. Michael was just being nice. But at least I wasn't alone anymore. Not completely, anyway. And I could feel good about that. My Dads would be happy about that too. Not that I was going to tell them, but ... whatever. At some point, I must have fallen asleep, because

the next thing I knew, the dazzle of morning was filling the tube with bright yellow light.

I must have been dazed, maybe it was the beer, but I felt like I was floating in a golden cloud. It must have been noticeable, a couple of other students even mentioned it, asking, "Are you all right? You look funny." One boy, one of the slighter ones, peered at me sideways. "You look like you just got laid."

"Nope, sorry." But I was smiling and it must have looked like a knowing smile to him, because he didn't believe me. "Okay, don't tell me," he said and walked away, obviously annoyed. I think I laughed a little, just not out loud.

It puzzled me, that I felt so good. Nothing really happened. We talked, we walked, we held hands, and the time passed without effort. It was...well, fun. But I'd never had fun like that before, so maybe that was why I was so...well, traumatized, but in a good way.

That evening, as the last of the afternoon faded toward dusk, I went out to the balcony with the clarinet again. I'd been thinking all day what I should play, I wanted something that would say how I felt, but without being too ...too something. I finally settled on an oldie called, "Fill Your Heart." It could be played fast and upbeat or slow and poignant. I opted for a slow beginning, then segued into a syncopated little dance. It worked. When I finally wailed into a triumphant cadenza, something I'd invented on my own, I felt exhilarated—and a voice from below hollered, "I'm coming up now!"

Michael bounced over the railing, I had no idea how he did that, with a bag of groceries slung over one shoulder. "Play that again," he said. "I'll fix dinner."

"Nuh-uh. For my first encore—"

He laughed.

I put the clarinet to my lips and played, this time "Rhapsody In Blue." The clarinet wail at the beginning is an instant attention getter, but the real joy is everything that follows after, the way it just joyously celebrates itself. I had to play my own abridged version, I didn't have an orchestra-program accompanying me, didn't want one anyway, I like finding the truth of the music myself.

By the time I finished, Michael had dinner on the table. I'd been playing with my eyes closed so I hadn't seen what he was doing. I didn't expect much, not on a student provision, but as simple as this was, it was more than I had expected. A salad, sausages, and baked beans, sweetcakes for dessert—and a sparkling cider to accompany it all.

I'd been eating rations. I hadn't realized how much I'd been missing real food.

I looked at it laid out on the table, looked at his beaming smile, then back to the table again, then back to him, and abruptly I couldn't speak. I didn't know what I was feeling, but it was overwhelming. Finally, "This is so good—what you did—thank you!"

He reached over and with his thumb, he wiped a tear from my cheek. "You've been alone too long, haven't you?"

I could barely nod.

He slid over next to me on the bench and put his arm around my shoulder and pulled me close to him. "It's all right. You're not alone anymore." After a moment, he added, "Your music is beautiful. I loved it."

"Sometimes..." It took me a minute to get the words out. "Sometimes, it's all I have. I've never been on my own before—I dunno, I guess I didn't realize how much..."

He didn't say anything. He just continued to hold me close while I sniffled with tears that wouldn't quite come. "I'm such a big baby," I said.

"Well, I think you're adorable—"

"Huh?"

"Because you feel things so intensely. Most people don't. I wish I could feel that intensely. I'm always pushing my feelings down—"

I pulled away so I could turn and look at him. "Uh-uh." I pointed to the table. "You just express your feelings differently."

"Mm," he said.

"We should eat."

"Yeah."

The plates had kept the food warm. I don't remember eating as much as I remember that I kept looking at his eyes. They were shining.

"You really have been alone, haven't you?"

"I didn't think so. I mean, my Dads had a lot of friends. We saw a lot of people all the time, mostly the same people, but—um, yeah, no, not like this. I never had my own friends—a friend of my own, I mean. I'm not making sense, am I?"

"You're making perfect sense."

"Tell me about you," I said.

"Large family. Very large. We were always doing things for other people. I think it was kind of a competition. It was um…the discipline we were in. Looking to see what other people need." He changed the subject then. "Are you studying music?"

"No. I mean, a little, yes. To keep in practice. But my major is eco-management."

"How does that work?"

"Design and build an ecology. Run it for a thousand years, see if it's stable or if it collapses or if it evolves into something else. It's complex, I think that's why I love it. You have to design a whole solar system, figure out the Goldilocks zone, the size of the planet, the shape of its orbit, if it has moons, how far off axis it's tilted, how long is its year, how long is its day, does it have a molten core and plate tectonics and volcanoes and what does that do to the atmosphere, what kind of atmosphere, what about ice caps and ocean currents, are the oceans fresh or salty, and what kind of seasons, all of that—before you can even start figuring out what kind of life it can support. I went with a proto-Earth, so I can have dinosaurs, but…if you want something in the now, you gotta backtrack all the way to the beginning to figure out how to make it inevitable. I'm talking too much, aren't I?"

Michael shook his head. "Uh-uh. It's fascinating." He nodded toward the empty plates, started gathering them. "It's getting cold out here, let's move inside?"

We sat on the bed and sipped at the last of the cider. "What are you studying?"

"You'll laugh."

"No, I won't."

"Companions."

"No, really?"

"Well, no. Not really. I'm studying human/machine relationships. How do we make companions more lifelike? So lifelike that they're indistinguishable from humans. And should we?"

I thought about that for a moment, thinking about Boobie and Toddy and Derry and Dix and … maybe a few others in the future?

"You had companions growing up, didn't you?"

I nodded. "I thought it was a good thing."

"It probably was. Look at how much you can do."

"And…look what I've been missing too."

Michael shook his head. "You really want to be like them?" He pointed his chin in the direction of the distant dorms.

"No." I had to laugh at that. "That life is so… shallow."

"Yeah."

We sat in silence for a while, side-by-side on my bed.

"Um...can I ask you something?"

He looked at me. "Sure."

"It's kind of personal."

"It's all right."

"Have you ever been with...I mean, have you ever done it? With a real person, I mean?"

Michael shook his head. "Uh-uh." He looked at his hands, still holding the glass of cider. "I'm kind of—you're not going to believe this—um, shy."

"Excuse me?" I laughed. "You come leaping up onto my balcony with a bag full of dinner... and you want me to believe you're shy?"

"I've been working on my shyness. Working on not letting it stop me."

"Well, yeah. Okay. Um. I think you, uh—I think you've pretty much handled it."

His turn to laugh. He said, "Um, it's a thing, a trick. If I recognize I'm reluctant to do something. Afraid. Then I do it. And then I don't have to be afraid of it anymore, do I?"

"Uh..." I closed my mouth. It made sense—a terrifying kind of sense. "So, you were afraid to talk to me?"

He nodded.

"What else are you afraid of?"

"If I say it, I'll have to do it."

"Well, then...say it."

Instead, he leaned forward and...kissed me. Just a tentative brush of his lips across mine. Barely a hint of a kiss. But the intention was clear.

He pulled back and looked at me, a question in his eyes. Was that all right?

My turn to lean forward. This kiss was a lot better. Exploration of the possibilities of kissing...

Wow. Raised to the power of infinity.

We separated just long enough to look at each other, then kissed again. This time, relaxing into the familiarity of it, allowing ourselves to sink completely and deeply into the sheer physical experience of tongues touching, dancing, tasting—

When we paused for breath, readjusting our positions on the couch, starting to unbutton each other's shirts, Michael's fingertip traced its way from the tip of my nose, down across my lips, to my chin, and at last my chest—the past disappeared. It was as if I'd never been touched before.

"I've never done it with another person before either."

"I kinda figured that. Well, hoped for it."

"Is that all right?"

He nodded hesitantly—and in that moment, I saw the shyness he had admitted. It was adorable. He said, "I guess it's a good thing then. We get to figure it out together, don't we?" He resumed unbuttoning my shirt, helped me take it off. I'd never let anyone undress me before, but for the first time I wasn't ashamed to be half-naked in front of another man.

He stroked my chest, my belly. He tugged at my belt. I stopped him so I could unbutton his shirt. When the last magnetic button parted, he shrugged it off and I looked at his naked torso as if I'd never seen a man before. "You're beautiful," I said.

He blushed, shook his head, blushed again, smiled, leaned forward, and we kissed so long I forgot what we were talking about. It didn't matter. The talk was just vibrations in air. The emotional vibrations were much more intense.

After a while, we took our pants off too.

And a little after that, our underwear.

I'd never been this naked before.

I'd never wanted to be this naked before.

He liked what he was seeing, so I wanted him to see it all. I liked him looking at me. I liked looking at him looking at me.

And then we rolled into each other's arms and it was amazing how well our bodies fit together. I matched my rhythm to his and he matched his to mine, and we rocked easily together as if we'd been made for this moment from the beginning.

It wasn't all sex. It wasn't sex at all. It was emotion. It was a little but of lust and a little bit of passion, but a great deal more of surrendering, opening, exploring, discovering, and a long slow tumble into enchantment.

We didn't rush, we weren't in a hurry—we didn't know where we were going, so we took our time getting there. Sometimes we'd stop, we'd look at each other, we'd catch our breath. Once, I got up to get a glass of ice water and we shared the ice in a kiss, pushing the last ice cube back and forth between us, feeling it melt until we were simply sharing a memory of coldness on our tongues.

I laid on top of him and felt his desire pressing up against me like a beacon, and then we rolled over and he was on top of me, and I could feel our hearts beating in unison, every lub-dub a wave pulsing outward from our mutual centers.

We wrestled for a bit, kissing all the different parts of each other's bodies. We could have done more, but we didn't need to—even this much was overwhelming. It all felt so...right. I felt complete.

And then, he was on top of me, and he said, "I'm getting close," and I said, "Me too," and we rocked together with a growing intensity. I wanted this to be perfect for him, so I matched his every movement, pushing hard against him with every thrust until that startling instant we both reached the finish line together, his completion triggered mine, and we surged together—

I lay there gasping for breath, listening to him breathing hard as well. Our hearts pounded between us, a staccato pumping of amazement. We had just gone through a door that wasn't there until we went through it.

Neither of us could speak, there was nothing to say. We just held onto each other forever.

Until finally, finally he lifted up and looked down at me, his eyes shining—I sparkled back at him.

"Wow," I said. "That was perfect."

Perfect.

The word hung between us like a sudden question.

Perfect?

I pushed him up far enough to look into his eyes, searching for evidence.

"What?" he asked.

"That was too perfect."

"Is that a problem?"

"Um—"

He frowned, just the slightest furrowing of his brow, the slightest narrowing of his eyes. "What?"

"Michael—"

"What?"

"Did my Dads send you? Are you a companion?"

He smiled gently and put a finger across my lips. "Shh," he said.

"No, tell me."

"I can't," he said. "We're not allowed to."

Was he joking? I couldn't tell.

Oh, what the hell. I pulled him down into another endless kiss.

DE-EXTINCTION EVENT

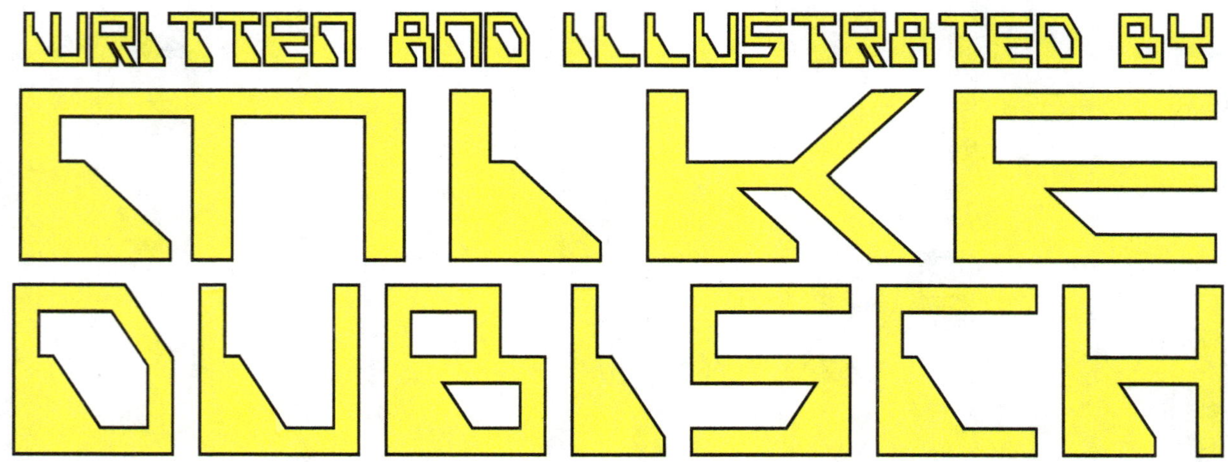

AT LAST! ONE OF THIS PAIR IS A PERFECT SPECIMEN.
DISPOSE OF IT, AS PER USUAL.
AND THE OTHER?

IT REMAINED HEALTHY LONGER, BUT ULTIMATELY WAS UNSTABLE.
THE STABLE CLONE?
WAKE HER.
WHERE—WHERE AM I?
GOOD MORNING EVA.
SUFFICE TO SAY YOU A VERY IMPORTANT TO US HERE. NOW IT'S TIME TO OPEN YOUR EYES.
WELL, THAT'S A LITTLE HARD TO EXPLAIN.

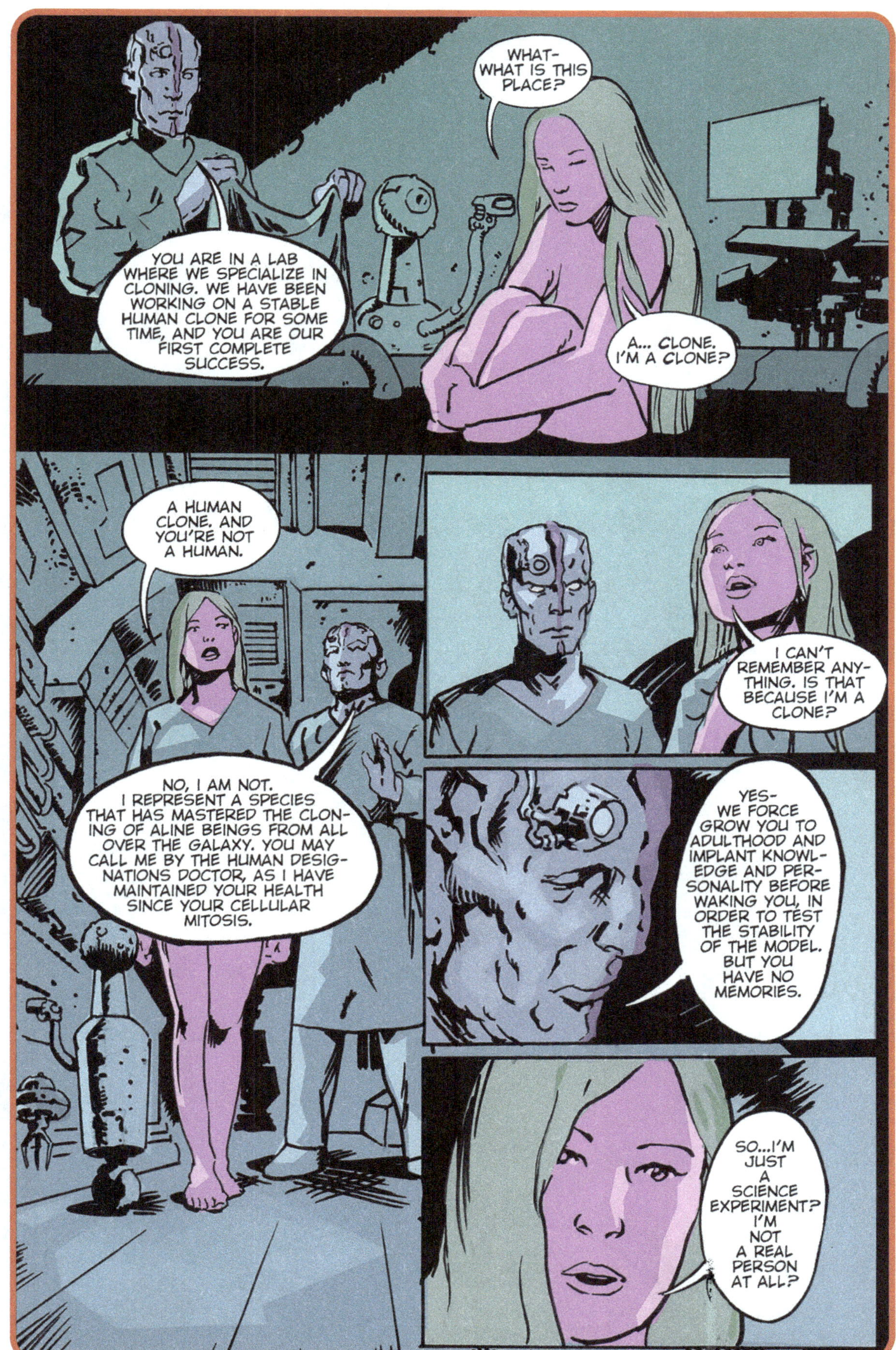

WHAT- WHAT IS THIS PLACE?
YOU ARE IN A LAB WHERE WE SPECIALIZE IN CLONING. WE HAVE BEEN WORKING ON A STABLE HUMAN CLONE FOR SOME TIME, AND YOU ARE OUR FIRST COMPLETE SUCCESS.
A... CLONE. I'M A CLONE?
A HUMAN CLONE. AND YOU'RE NOT A HUMAN.
I CAN'T REMEMBER ANY-THING. IS THAT BECAUSE I'M A CLONE?
NO, I AM NOT. I REPRESENT A SPECIES THAT HAS MASTERED THE CLON-ING OF ALINE BEINGS FROM ALL OVER THE GALAXY. YOU MAY CALL ME BY THE HUMAN DESIG-NATIONS DOCTOR, AS I HAVE MAINTAINED YOUR HEALTH SINCE YOUR CELLULAR MITOSIS.
YES- WE FORCE GROW YOU TO ADULTHOOD AND IMPLANT KNOWL-EDGE AND PER-SONALITY BEFORE WAKING YOU, IN ORDER TO TEST THE STABILITY OF THE MODEL. BUT YOU HAVE NO MEMORIES.
SO...I'M JUST A SCIENCE EXPERIMENT? I'M NOT A REAL PERSON AT ALL?

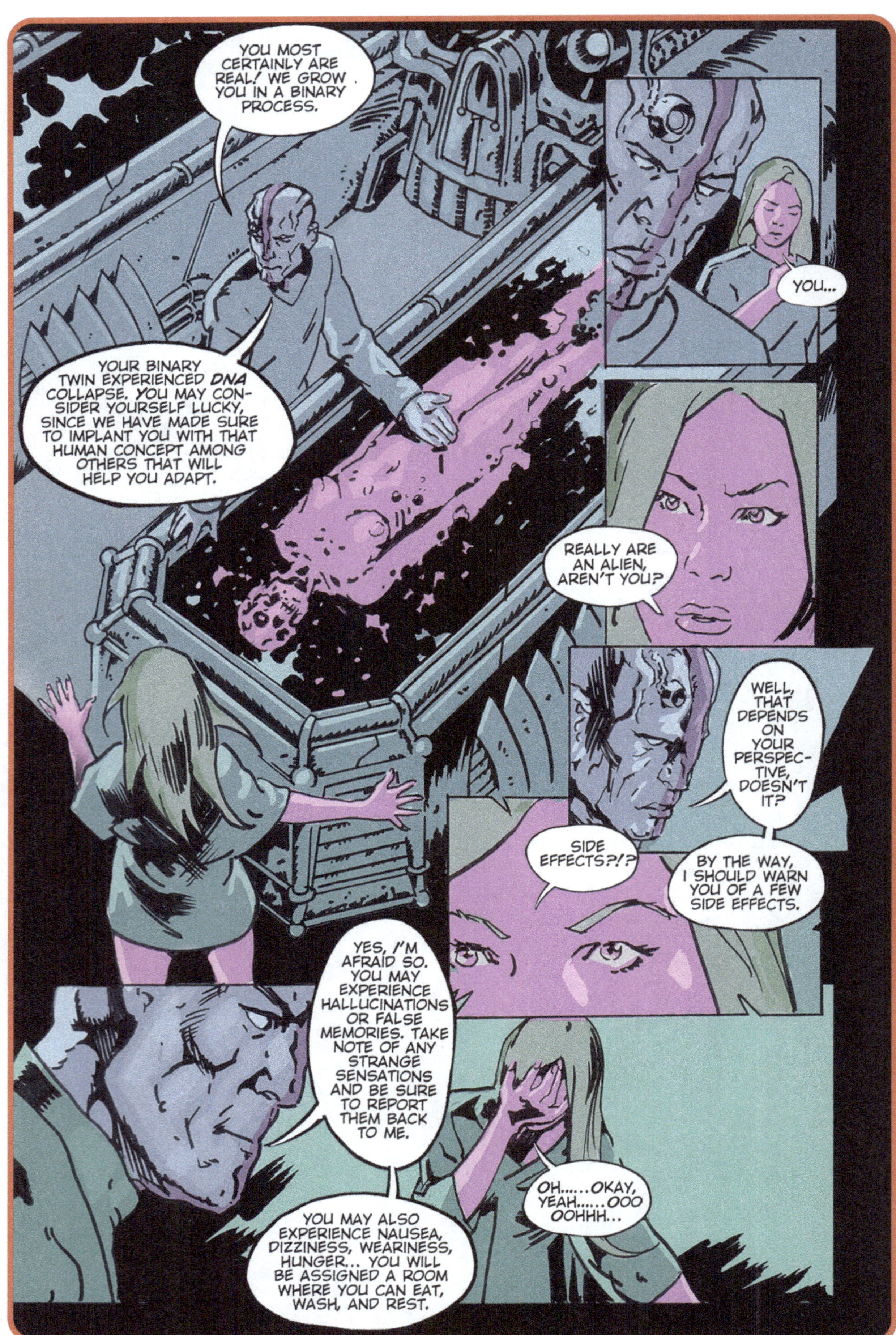

YOU MOST CERTAINLY ARE REAL! WE GROW YOU IN A BINARY PROCESS.

YOU...

YOUR BINARY TWIN EXPERIENCED DNA COLLAPSE. YOU MAY CONSIDER YOURSELF LUCKY, SINCE WE HAVE MADE SURE TO IMPLANT YOU WITH THAT HUMAN CONCEPT AMONG OTHERS THAT WILL HELP YOU ADAPT.

REALLY ARE AN ALIEN, AREN'T YOU?

WELL, THAT DEPENDS ON YOUR PERSPECTIVE, DOESN'T IT?

BY THE WAY, I SHOULD WARN YOU OF A FEW SIDE EFFECTS.

SIDE EFFECTS?!?

YES, I'M AFRAID SO. YOU MAY EXPERIENCE HALLUCINATIONS OR FALSE MEMORIES. TAKE NOTE OF ANY STRANGE SENSATIONS AND BE SURE TO REPORT THEM BACK TO ME.

OH......OKAY, YEAH......OOO OOHHH...

YOU MAY ALSO EXPERIENCE NAUSEA, DIZZINESS, WEARINESS, HUNGER... YOU WILL BE ASSIGNED A ROOM WHERE YOU CAN EAT, WASH, AND REST.

HOW WEIRD IS THIS?
I'M A CLONE GROWN IN AN ALIEN'S TEST TUBE AND I JUST ATE WHAT WAS PROBABLY MY FIRST SOLID FOOD.
AND I'M SPLASHING WATER ON MY FACE BECAUSE I KNOW IT WILL REFRESH ME...
BUT I CAN'T REMEMBER WHY I KNOW THAT!
GET A GRIP EVA! IT'S NOT SO BAD. YOU JUST NEED TO FIND OUT WHY THEY MADE YOU- WHAT ARE YOU?
WAIT, WHAT THE?!?
MY HAIR! MY FINGER-NAILS!

NO, WAIT- CALM DOWN. THIS IS NOT REAL.
JUST FOCUS.
THE DOCTOR SAID THERE MIGHT BE HAL- LUCINATIONS.
THIS IS THE HALLUCINATION YOU CLONE BITCH!
OKAY.
NOTE TAKEN.
I AM EXPERIENCING STRANGE SENSATIONS. I NEED TO SEE MY DOCTOR RIGHT AWAY.

DOCTOR! WHAT'S HAPPENING TO ME?!?
UH OH.
THIS LOOKS SERIOUS.
MY HAIR AND NAILS ARE GROWING OUT OF CONTROL! MY HAIR EVEN SEEMS TO MOVE WITH A MIND OF ITS OWN!
LET'S TAKE A CLOSER LOOK AT WHAT'S HAPPENING.
YES, AS I SUSPECTED.
YOUR DNA IS NOT AS STABLE AS I HAD HOPED. ONCE ACTIVE OUTSIDE THE GROWING CHAMBER, SOME OF THE EXTRATERRESTRIAL BUILDING BLOCKS I HAD TO USE TO COMPLETE YOUR DECIMATED GENOME HAS BEGUN TO STRIVE FOR DOMINANCE.

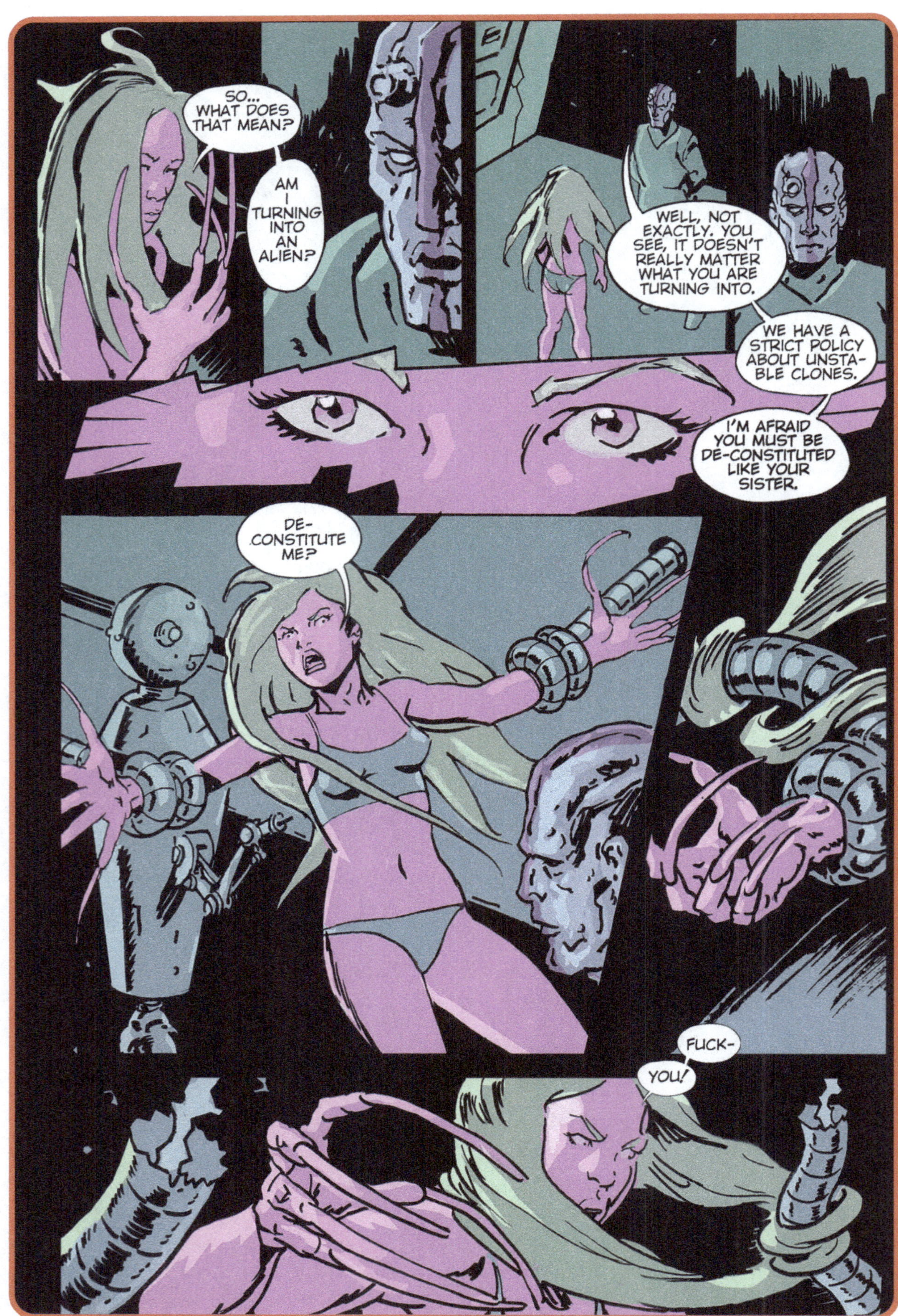
SO... WHAT DOES THAT MEAN?
AM I TURNING INTO AN ALIEN?
WELL, NOT EXACTLY. YOU SEE, IT DOESN'T REALLY MATTER WHAT YOU ARE TURNING INTO.
WE HAVE A STRICT POLICY ABOUT UNSTABLE CLONES.
I'M AFRAID YOU MUST BE DE-CONSTITUTED LIKE YOUR SISTER.
DE-CONSTITUTE ME?
FUCK-YOU!

HEY ASSHOLE!
AND IT TURNS OUT ONE OF THE THINGS I CAN'T REMEMBER......
STILL THINK YOU CAN JUST... DE-CONSTITUTE ME?
WELL, I'M STILL HUMAN ENOUGH FOR THAT TO PISS ME OFF!
IS WHY EXACTLY I SHOULDN'T KILL YOUR ASS!
SO... WHAT'S YOUR DIAGNOSIS...
DOCTOR?
OH SHIT.

WHAT KIND OF
MONSTER AM I
BECOMING?!?

MY BODY'S STILL MUTATING!
I'VE GOT TO GET OUT OF HERE!
THE OUTSIDE!

IT'S AMAZING..
SO BEAUTIFUL...
THEY'VE CLONED SO
MANY EARTH PLANTS
AND ANIMALS

BUT, WHY? WHY HAVE THEY DONE ALL THIS?
ARGGH! I'VE GROWN TOO BIG. MY BODY IS CRUSHING MY HEART. I'M DYING!
WHAT'S THAT!?!
OH NO! NO!

THE GRAVITY IN THE BIO-RING WAS TOO MUCH FOR HER INCREASED SIZE.
NO, WE MUST KEEP FOCUSING ON DEVELOPING A STABLE HUMAN CLONE. THAT IS THE ULTIMATE GOAL OF RESURRECTION BIOLOGY.
THE EXPERIMENT MIGHT PERHAPS LAST LONGER IF PLACED IN A LOWER G.
THE HUMANS WERE A MOST INTER-ESTING AND DYNAMIC SPECIES. WE WILL KEEP STRIVING FOR THEIR REVIVAL.

CREDITS

DAVID GERROLD has been writing professionally for half a century. He created the tribbles for "Star Trek" and the Sleestaks for "**Land Of The Lost**." His most famous novel is "**The Man Who Folded Himself**." His semi-autobiographical tale of his son's adoption, "**The Martian Child**" won both the Hugo and the Nebula awards, and was the basis for the 2007 movie star ring John Cusack and Amanda Peet. He is the 2022 winner of the Heinlein award for out standing published works in science fiction and technical writings that inspire the human exploration of space.

ANDRE ALICE NORTON (born Alice Mary Norton, February 17, 1912 – March 17, 2005) was an American writer of science fiction and fantasy works. She wrote under the names Andre Norton, Andrew North, and Allen Weston and was the first woman to be inducted by the Science Fiction and Fantasy Hall of Fame.

CHRIS FARMER is a writer from Chilt, Washington. Steeped in his mother's science fiction collection, he has always wanted to write the great american novel, and never got around to it. Instead he doodles, and writes short stories.

ANNA TAMBOUR is also a photographer of the unnoticed. Her new story collection **Death Goes to the Dogs** was published April 2023.

FRED GOLT has been designing street signs for the past five decades under another alias. Now, shifting gears with my first writing debut in Forbidden Futures.

MIKE DUBISCH has designed characters and illustrated windows into multiple universes, from **Star Wars** to **Dungeons and Dragons, Aliens VS Predator, The Wheel Of Time**, and the **Cthulhu Mythos**. In **Forbidden Futures** magazine, Mike collaborates with the world's greatest genre fiction writers to help create new universes every issue. A veteran of role playing games, underground horror comix, pulp science fiction magazines and role playing game miniatures, Mike has been a professional illustrator for over three decades, and is known as a visionary fantasy illustrator, surrealist and graphic novelist.

CODY GOODFELLOW has written nine novels and five collections of short stories. His writing has been favored with three Wonderland Book Awards. His comics work has been featured in **Mystery Meat, Creepy, Slow Death Zero** and **Skin Crawl**. As an actor, he has appeared in numerous short films, TV shows, music videos by Anthrax and Beck, and a Days Inn commercial. He also wrote, co-produced and scored the Lovecraftian hygiene films **Baby Got Bass** and **Stay At Home Dad**, which can be viewed on YouTube. He lives in San Diego, California.

ODDNESS (author, publisher, producer) originates from unknown lands, and dabbles in modular synths and playing video games.

www.ingramcontent.com/pod-product-compliance
Lightning Source LLC
Chambersburg PA
CBHW080911190726
48294CB00008B/2055